For Danielle Darrieux

Christmas 2010

This is a book, a life in a book everyone should read. Easy and so intense... with all my love I wish you all the best....

OSCAR and the LADY IN PINK

Re

by

Eric-Emmanuel Schmitt

translated by

Adriana Hunter

First published in France as *Oscar et la dame rose* by Éditions Albin Michel, S.A., 2002.

First published in hardback in English in Great Britain in 2005 by Atlantic Books, an imprint of Grove Atlantic Limited.

This paperback edition published in Great Britain in 2008 by Atlantic Books.

2 3 4 5 6 7 8 9

A CIP catalogue record for this book is available from the British Library.

ISBN 978 184354 886 7

Design by Lindsay Nash

Printed in Great Britain

Atlantic Books
An imprint of Grove Atlantic Ltd
Ormond House
26–27 Boswell Street
London WC1N 3JZ

Dear God

My name's Oscar, I'm ten years old, and I set fire to the bloody cat, the dog, the house (I even think I fried the goldfish) and this is the first letter I've ever written to you because, up till now, I didn't have time because of school.

I'd better warn you straight away: I hate writing. Someone really has to force me. Because writing's fluffy, sissy, frilly, prissy, et cetera. Writing's just a lie to make things look better. A grown-up thing.

And I can prove it, I mean, look at the beginning of my letter: 'My name's Oscar, I'm ten years old, and I set fire to the bloody cat, the dog, the house (I even think I fried the goldfish) and this is the first letter I've ever written to you because, up till now, I didn't have time because of school.' I could just as easily have put: 'People call me Egghead, I only look about seven, I live in hospital because I've got cancer and I've never spoken to you because I don't even believe you exist.'

Only, if I put that, that would muck everything up, you wouldn't be so interested in me. And, you see, I need you to be interested.

Actually, what would be really good would be if you could do me a couple of favours.

I'll explain.

Hospital's a really friendly place with loads of cheerful grown-ups talking quite openly, and loads of toys and ladies in pink who want to play with the children, and friends who are always free – like Bacon, Einstein and Popcorn. Basically, hospital's brilliant if you're the sort of patient who makes everyone happy.

But I don't make anyone happy any more. Ever since I

had my bone marrow transplant I can tell I'm not making them happy any more. When Dr Düsseldorf examines me in the morning his heart's not really in it, he's disappointed with me. He looks at me and doesn't say anything as if I've done something wrong. But I really tried hard with the operation, you know: I was good, I let them put me to sleep, it didn't cry when it hurt, I took all the pills. Sometimes I feel like shouting at him, like telling him it could be him – Dr Düsseldorf with his black eyebrows – who got the operation wrong. But he looks so unhappy that my insults stick in my throat. The longer Dr Düsseldorf goes on looking miserable and saying nothing, the more guilty I feel. I realise I've become a bad patient, the sort of patient who means you can't keep saying how wonderful the medical profession is.

And what the doctor thinks is contagious. Everyone on the floor looks at me like that now – the nurses, the housemen, the cleaners. They look sad when I'm in a good mood, and they force themselves to laugh when I make a joke. It's true, no one laughs like before.

Granny Rose's the only one who hasn't changed. If you ask me, she's too old to change anyway. And she's just too Granny Rose as well. I don't need to introduce you to Granny Rose, God, she's a good friend of yours, seeing she's the one who told me to write to you. The problem is I'm the only person who calls her Granny Rose. So you'll have to make a bit of an effort to see who I mean: you know the women in rosy-pink uniforms who come in to spend time with sick children, well she's the oldest one of all.

'How old are you, Granny Rose?'

'Can you remember thirteen-figure numbers, Oscar, my little man?'

'Oh! You must be joking!'

'No. But they really mustn't find out how old I am here, or they'll chuck me out and we won't see each other again.'

'Why?'

'I have to smuggle myself in. There's an age limit for the ladies in pink. And I'm way past it.'

'Past your sell-by date?'

'Yes.'

'Like a yoghurt?'

'Shush!'

'OK! I won't say a thing.'

She was really brave to admit her secret to me. But she chose the right person. I won't breathe a word. Mind you I think that – given all her wrinkles, fanning out like sunbeams round her eyes – it's incredible no one else has guessed.

Another time I found out one of her other secrets, and with this one I'm sure you'll be able to identify her, God.

We were walking round the hospital grounds and she stepped in a pooh.

'Shit!'

'Granny Rose, that's a swear word.'

'Hey, give me a bloody break, littl'un, I'll say what I like.'

'Granny Rose!!'

'And move your arse. We're meant to be walking, not having a snail race.'

When we stopped to sit on a bench and suck a sweet, I asked her:

'How come you speak like that?'

'It was my job, Oscar, my little man. In my line of work I'd have had it if I spoke too nicely.'

'And what was your work?'

'You're not going to believe me ...'

'I swear I'll believe you.'

'Wrestling.'

'I don't believe you!'

'Wrestling! they called me the Languedoc Strangler.'

Ever since, when I'm feeling a bit down and she's sure no one else can hear, Granny Rose tells me about her big fights: the Languedoc Strangler against the Butcher of Limousin, her twenty-year struggle with Diabolica Sinclair, a Dutch woman who had bombshells instead of boobs, and most of all the world-cup fight against Ulla-Ulla who was known as the Bitch of Buchenwald and who'd never been beaten, even by Thighs of Steel – she was Granny Rose's role model when she was a wrestler.

It's like a fantasy for me when I think about her fights because I imagine her in the ring as she is now, a little old lady in a pink uniform, a bit unsteady on her feet, beating the hell out of these ogres in swimming costumes. I feel as if it's me. I become the strongest and the best. I get my revenge.

Right, so Granny Rose or the Languedoc Strangler. If you can't work out who Granny Rose is with all those clues, God, then you'd better stop being God and retire. Is that clear?

Let's get back to me.

Basically, people here were really disappointed with my transplant. My chemo was disappointing too but that didn't matter so much because they could still put their hope in the transplant. Now I get the feeling the doctors don't know what to suggest, I even think they feel sorry for me. Dr Düsseldorf (who Mummy thinks is gorgeous even though I'd say he's done a bit well in the eyebrow department) looks so sad, like a Father Christmas who's got no more presents left in his sack.

And things are getting worse. I've talked to my friend Bacon about it. He's not really called Bacon, he's Yves but we call him Bacon because it suits him so much better, given how badly he's burned.

'Bacon, I feel like the doctors don't like me any more, they find me depressing.'

'Rubbish, Egghead! Doctors are like re-chargeable batteries. They've always got loads of ideas for operations they can do on you. I've worked out they've promised to do at least six on me.'

'Maybe they find you inspiring.'

'I suppose they must.'

'But why don't they just tell me I'm going to die?'

Then Bacon did what everyone in hospital does: he went deaf. If you say 'die' in hospital, no one hears it. You can guarantee there'll be a pause and then they'll talk about something else. I've tried it out on everyone. Except Granny Rose.

So this morning I wanted to see if she got a bit hard of hearing at that precise moment like everyone else.

'Granny Rose, I feel like no one's telling me I'm going to die.'

She looks at me. Is she going to do what all the others do? Please, Languedoc Strangler, don't give in, look after your ears!

'Why would you want people to tell you, Oscar, if you already know!'

Phew, she heard.

'You see, Granny Rose, it's as if they've invented another hospital instead of this one which really exists. They pretend you only go to hospital to get better. But really you come here to die too.'

'You're right, Oscar. And I think we make the same mistake with life. We forget how fragile life is, how brittle and short-lived. We all behave as if we're immortal.'

'My operation didn't work, did it, Granny Rose?'

Granny Rose didn't answer. That was her way of saying no. When she was sure I understood, she came right over and pleaded:

'Obviously, I didn't tell you anything. Do you promise?'

'Promise.'

We didn't say anything for a bit. I mean, we had a lot of new ideas to get used to.

'Why don't you write to God, Oscar?'

'Oh no, not you too, Granny Rose!'

'Not me what?'

'Not you! I thought you weren't a liar.'

'But I haven't lied to you.'

'Well, why are you talking about God, then? They've already done the Father Christmas routine on me. Once was enough!'

'Oscar, there's no connection between God and Father Christmas.'

'There is. Same story. Brainwashing & Co.!'

'Do you really think that I, a former wrestler who won 160 fights out of 165 (and 43 of those were with knock-outs), that I, the Strangler of Languedoc, believe in Father Christmas for one second?'

'No.'

'Well then, I don't believe in Father Christmas but I do

believe in God. There!'

Obviously, when she put it like that, it changed everything.

'And why would I want to write to God?'

'You wouldn't feel so lonely.'

'Not so lonely with someone who doesn't exist?'

'Make him exist.'

She leant over to me.

'Every time you believe in him, he'll exist a bit more. If you keep at it, he'll exist completely. Then, he'll do you good.'

'What could I write to him about?'

'Let him know what you're thinking. The things you don't say – they're the things that weigh on you, they take a hold, wear you down, paralyse you. They take all the room you need for new ideas, and start rotting inside you. You're going to become a dump for old ideas and you'll start smelling if you don't talk.'

'OK.'

'And the other thing with God is you can ask him for something every day. Just one thing, mind you!'

'He's rubbish, your God, Granny Rose. Aladdin got to have three wishes with the genie in the lamp.'

'One wish a day is better than three in a lifetime, isn't it?'

'OK. So can I order anything from him? Toys, sweets, a car ...'

'No, Oscar. God isn't Father Christmas. You can only ask for things for the mind.'

'Like?'

'Like: courage, patience, understanding.'

'OK. I see.'

'And, Oscar, you could also suggest favours to him for the others.'

'One wish a day, Granny Rose, don't muck about – I'm going to keep them for myself first!'

And that was that. So, God, with this first letter I've given you an idea of the sort of life I have here at the hospital (where they now look at me like some sort of obstacle to the medical profession), and I'd like to ask you to clear something up for me: Am I going to get better?

Just answer yes or no. It's not very complicated. Yes or no.

Delete where not applicable.

Till tomorrow, love
Oscar

PS I don't know your address, what should I do?

Dear God

Wow! You're pretty good. Before I even posted the letter, you gave me an answer. How did you do it?

This morning I was playing chess with Einstein in the games room when Popcorn came to tell me:

'Your parents are here.'

'My parents? They can't be. They only come on Sundays.'

'I saw their car, a red Jeep with a white cover.'

'It can't be.'

I shrugged my shoulders and carried on playing with Einstein. But, because I was preoccupied, Einstein kept nicking all my pieces, and that wound me up even more. We don't call him Einstein because he's more intelligent than the others but because his head's twice the size of anyone else's. Apparently it's got water inside. It's a shame, if it'd all been brains, Einstein could have been amazing.

When I saw I was going to lose, I gave up on the game and followed Popcorn into his room which overlooks the car park. He was right: my parents were here.

I should tell you, God, that we live a long way apart, my parents and me. I didn't realise it when I lived there but, now that I don't, it really seems a long way. So that's why my parents can only come once a week, on Sundays, because they don't work on Sundays. No, and nor do I.

'You see, I was right,' Popcorn said. 'How much are you going to give me for coming to tell you?'

'I've got some hazelnut chocolates.'

'Haven't you got any more of those strawberry things?'

'No.'

'OK, I'll go for the chocolates then.'

Obviously, we're not allowed to give Popcorn food, given that he's here to lose weight. 99kg at nine years old, he's 1.10m tall and about the same across! The only piece of clothing he can get all of himself into is an American polo shirt. And even then the stripes get a bit sea-sick. To be honest, none of us thinks he'll ever stop being fat and he makes us feel so sorry for him because he gets terribly hungry, so we always give him our left-overs. One chocolate's such a tiny thing compared to that great mass of blubber! If we're wrong then the nurses had better stop ramming him full of suppositories too.

I went back to my room to wait for my parents. At first I didn't really notice the time passing because I was short of breath, then I realised that they'd had more than enough time to get to my room, much more.

I suddenly guessed where they were. I slipped out into the corridor and, when no one was looking, I went down the stairs, then I walked through the gloom to Dr Düsseldorf's office.

Bingo! They were there. I could hear their voices

through the door. I was so tired out from walking that it took me a few seconds to get my heart back in its place, and that's when everything went wrong. I heard something I wasn't meant to hear. My mother was sobbing and Dr Düsseldorf kept saying: 'We've tried everything, please believe me, we've tried everything', and my father replied in this strangulated voice: 'I'm sure you have, Dr Düsseldorf, I'm sure you have.'

I stayed there with my ear glued to that iron door. I don't know what was colder, me or the metal.

Then Dr Düsseldorf said:

'Would you like to go and give him a cuddle?'

'I wouldn't have the strength,' said my mother.

'He mustn't see us in this state,' added my father.

And that's when I realised that my parents were both cowards. Worse than that: they were cowards who thought I was a coward!

I heard chairs scraping, so I guessed they were going to come out, and I opened the first door I could find.

That's how I ended up in the broom cupboard which is

where I spent the rest of the morning because, you may not know this, God, but broom cupboards open from the outside, not the inside – as if people were worried that the brushes and buckets and mops might run away in the night!

Anyway, it didn't bother me being shut up in the dark because I didn't feel like seeing anyone any more, and because my arms and legs weren't really working properly after the shock it gave me, hearing what I heard.

Round about midday, I could tell there was quite a commotion going on upstairs. I could hear footsteps, running. Then people started shouting my name all over the place:

'Oscar! Oscar!'

It felt good hearing people calling me and not answering. I felt like being a pain to the whole world.

After that, I think I must have slept for a bit, then I made out the sound of Mrs N'da dragging her clogs – she's the cleaning lady. She opened the door and then we really scared each other, we both screamed so loudly, her because she wasn't expecting to find me there, and me because I'd forgotten she was so black. Or that she could scream so loudly.

After that there was a hell of a scrum. They all came running, Dr Düsseldorf, the charge nurse, the duty nurses, the other cleaners. I thought they'd be angry with me, but they went all stupid about it, and I soon realised I should make the most of the situation, straight away.

'I want to see Granny Rose.'

'But where were you, Oscar? How are you feeling?'

'I want to see Granny Rose.'

'How did you end up in this cupboard? Did you follow someone? Did you hear anything?'

'I want to see Granny Rose.'

'Have a glass of water.'

'No. I want to see Granny Rose.'

'Have a mouthful of ...'

'No. I want to see Granny Rose.'

Hard as granite. A cliff-face. A block of concrete. Nothing doing. I wasn't even listening to what they were saying any more. I wanted to see Granny Rose.

Dr Düsseldorf looked very put-out in front of all the others because he had absolutely no control over me. In the end he gave in.

'Will someone go and get this woman!'

Then I agreed to rest, and I slept for a bit in my room.

When I woke up, Granny Rose was there. She was smiling.

'Well done, Oscar, you got what you wanted. You gave them a hell of a slap in the face. But the net result is they're jealous of me now.'

'I don't give a monkey's.'

'They're good people, Oscar. Really good people.'

'I don't give a monkey's.'

'What is it, what's wrong?'

'Dr Düsseldorf told my parents I was going to die and they ran away. I hate them.'

I told her everything, in detail, like I have for you, God.

'Mmm,' said Granny Rose, 'that reminds me of my fight in Béthune against Wham Bam Sarah, the wrestler who oiled her whole body, the eel of the wrestling ring. She was a real acrobat and she fought almost naked, and she slipped out of your hands when you tried to get her in a hold. She only ever fought in Béthune and she won the Béthune Cup every year. But, you see, I really wanted it, that Béthune Cup!'

'What did you do, Granny Rose?'

'Some friends of mine threw flour over her as she came into the ring. Oil and flour – it makes very good bread-crumbs! Three flips and two swift moves, and Wham Bam Sarah was on the carpet. After I'd dealt with her, they didn't call her the eel of the ring any more, but the breaded cod!'

'I'm sorry, Granny Rose, but I don't really see the connection.'

'Well, I can see it perfectly. There's always a solution, Oscar, there's always a bag of flour somewhere. You should write to God. He's better than me.'

'Even at wrestling?'

'Yes. God even knows a thing or two about wrestling. Have a go, my little man. What's upsetting you the most?'

'I hate my parents.'

'Well then, you've got to really hate them.'

'I didn't think you were going to say that!'

'Well, I have said it. Really hate them. It'll give you something to get your teeth into. And when you've had a really good gnaw at it, when you've polished it off, you'll realise it wasn't worth it. Tell God about all this, in your letter. Ask him to come and see you.'

'Does he move about?'

'In his own way. Not very often. It's actually quite rare.'

'Why? Is he ill too?'

And when Granny Rose sighed then I realised she didn't want to admit it to me but you're in a pretty bad state too, God.

'Haven't your parents ever talked to you about God, Oscar?'

'Forget it. My parents are stupid.'

'Of course they are, but haven't they ever talked to you about God?'

'Yes. Just once. To say they didn't believe in him. They

only believe in Father Christmas.'

'Are they really that stupid, Oscar, my little man?'

'You have no idea! The day I came home from school saying they had to stop mucking about, that – like all my friends – I knew Father Christmas didn't exist, they looked devastated. I was angry they'd made me look stupid in the playground, so they swore they'd never tried to trick me and that they had honestly believed in Father Christmas too, and that they were really disappointed, no but I mean really disappointed to find out he wasn't real! A couple of complete idiots, I tell you, Granny Rose!'

'So they don't believe in God?'

'No.'

'And that's never intrigued you?'

'If I worried about what stupid people think, I wouldn't have time for what intelligent people think.'

'You're right. But the fact that your parents, who – according to you – are stupid ...'

'Yes, really stupid, Granny Rose!'

'So, if your parents who are wrong don't believe in him,

then don't you think you should believe in him and ask him to come and see you?'

'All right. But didn't you say he was bedridden?'

'No. He's got a very special way of seeing people. He comes to see you in thought. In your mind.'

Now, I really liked that. I thought that was very clever. Then Granny Rose added:

'You'll see: his visits do a lot of good.'

'OK. I'll talk to him about it. Mind you, at the moment, it's your visits that do me the most good.'

Granny Rose smiled and she leaned over, almost shyly, to give me a kiss on the cheek. She didn't dare go all the way. She asked for permission with her eyes.

'Go on. Kiss me. I won't tell the others. I don't want to ruin your reputation as a wrestler.'

She touched my cheek with her lips, and it felt nice, it made me feel warm and a bit tingly, with a smell of powder and soap.

'When are you coming again?'

'I'm only allowed to come twice a week.'

'Oh no, that's hopeless, Granny Rose! I'm not going to wait three days!'

'It's the rule.'

'Who makes the rules?'

'Dr Düsseldorf.'

'Right now Dr Düsseldorf poohs his pants every time he sees me. Go and ask him for permission, Granny Rose. I'm not joking.'

She looked at me, hesitating.

'I'm not joking. If you don't come and see me every day, I won't write to God.'

'I'll try.'

Granny Rose left and I started to cry.

I hadn't realised, before, just how badly I needed help. I hadn't realised, before, just how ill I was. When I thought about not seeing Granny Rose any more, I suddenly understood, and then there it all was streaming down my face in tears, burning my cheeks.

Luckily, I had a bit of time to pull myself together before she came back.

'It's sorted: I've got permission. I can come and see you every day for twelve days.'

'Just me.'

'Just you, Oscar. Twelve days.'

And I don't know what got into me then but the tears came back and made me shake all over. And I know that boys shouldn't cry, specially not me with my egghead which means I don't look like a boy or a girl but more like a Martian. There was nothing for it, though. I couldn't stop myself.

'Twelve days? Are things really that bad, Granny Rose?'

She was itching to cry too. She was teetering. The wrestler in her was stopping the little girl in her from letting go. It was nice to watch and it took my mind off things a bit.

'What day is it, Oscar?'

'What do you think? Can't you see my calendar? It's the 19th of December.'

'Where I come from, Oscar, there's a local legend which says that in the last twelve days of the year you can work out what the weather will be like over the twelve months of the year to come. You just have to watch each day, and that gives you a miniature version of a month. The 19th of December represents the month of January, the 20th, February, and so on until the 31st of December which predicts the following month of December.'

'Is it true?'

'It's a legend. The legend of the twelve divinations. I'd like us to play it. Well, mostly you. Starting today, you'll treat each day as if it counted for ten years.'

'Ten years?'

'Yes. One day: ten years.'

'So, in twelve days' time, I'll be a hundred and thirty!'

'Yes, can you imagine it?'

Granny Rose kissed me – she's taking a liking to that, I can tell – then she left.

So, there it is, God: this morning I was born, and I didn't really notice; things got a bit clearer towards midday when I was five years old, I became more aware but it wasn't to hear very good news; this evening I'm ten years old, the age of reason. I'll make the most of it to ask you for something: when you've got something to tell me like you did today, when I was five, can you make it not quite so harsh. Thanks.

Till tomorrow, love
Oscar

PS I've got something to ask you. I know I only get to have one wish a day, but that wish just now was only a little wish, more like advice.

I'd be on for a little visit. A mind-visit. I think that's very clever. I'd really like it if you paid me one of those visits. I'm open from eight in the morning till nine in the evening. The rest of the time I'm sleeping. Sometimes I even have a little sleep during the day, because of the treatments. But if you find me napping, please feel free to wake me up. It would be stupid to miss each other by a couple of minutes, wouldn't it?

Dear God

Today I went through my teenage years and it wasn't a very smooth ride. What a hassle! I had loads of problems with my friends, my parents and everything because of girls. I'm not sorry to be twenty this evening because I can say, phew, the worst of it's behind me. Puberty, blimey! I wouldn't want to go through that again!

First of all, God, I'd like to point out that you didn't come. I got very little sleep today what with all the puberty problems I had, so I can't have missed you. And anyway, like I said, if I'm napping, give me a shake.

When I woke up Granny Rose was already here. During breakfast she told me about her fights with Dragon Breast, a Belgian wrestler who swallowed three kilos of raw meat a day and washed them down with a barrel of beer. Apparently Dragon Breast's real strength was her breath because of all the beer and meat fermenting together, and that was enough to knock some of her opponents out on its own. To beat her, Granny Rose had to come up with a new tactic: she wore a hood dipped in lavender and called herself the Carpentras Slayer. She always said wrestling needs muscles in your head too.

'Who do you really like, Oscar?'

'Here? At the hospital?'

'Yes.'

'Bacon, Einstein, Popcorn.'

'What about the girls?'

That stumped me, that question. I didn't want to answer. But Granny Rose was waiting and, faced with an international-standard wrestler, you can't mess around for ever.

'Peggy Blue.'

Peggy Blue is the blue girl. She lives in the second last room at the end of the corridor. She's got a kind smile but she hardly ever talks. She's like a fairy who's just come to hospital for a bit of a rest. She's got some complicated illness, the blue disease, a problem with blood which should be going to her lungs but doesn't, and that ends up making her skin this bluish colour. She's waiting for an operation which will make her pink. I think it's a shame, I think Peggy Blue's beautiful all in blue. She's surrounded by light and silence, it's like going into a chapel when you go near her.

'Have you told her?'

'I'm not going to go and stand there and say "Peggy Blue, I really like you."'

'You could. Why don't you?'

'I don't even know if she knows I exist.'

'Another good reason.'

'But look at me! She'd have to be keen on extraterrestrials, and I'm not sure she is.'

'Well, I think you're very handsome, Oscar.'

That was a bit of a conversation–stopper from Granny Rose. It's nice hearing that sort of thing, it makes all your hairs stand up, but you don't know how to reply.

'I don't want her to like me just for the way I look, Granny Rose.'

'How does she make you feel?'

'I want to protect her from the ghosts.'

'What? Are there ghosts here?'

'Yes. Every night. They wake us up and we don't know why. They hurt us because they pinch us, and they frighten us because we can't see them. Then it's difficult getting back to sleep.'

'Do you get them often, these ghosts?'

'No. Sleep's probably the thing I'm best at. But Peggy Blue, I sometimes hear her crying in the night. I'd like to protect her.'

'Go and tell her.'

'I couldn't really do it, anyway, because at night we're not allowed to leave our rooms. It's the rule.'

'Do the ghosts know the rules? No, I'm sure they don't. Be clever: if they hear you saying you're going to watch over Peggy Sue to protect her from them, then they won't dare come this evening.'

'Yeah, right ...'

'How old are you, Oscar?'

'I don't know. What's the time?'

'Ten o'clock. You're heading for fifteen. Don't you think it's time you trusted in your own feelings?'

At ten thirty I made up my mind and walked all the way to the door of her room – it was open.

'Hello, Peggy, it's Oscar.'

She was lying delicately on her bed, she looked like Snow White waiting for the prince when those stupid dwarves think she's dead. Snow White like those photos of snow when the snow's blue and not white.

She turned to look at me and I wondered then whether she would see me as the prince or one of the dwarves. I would tick the box next to 'dwarf' because of my egghead, but she didn't say anything, and that's what's really good about Peggy Blue: she never says anything and everything stays all mysterious.

'I've come to tell you that this evening, and every evening from now on, if you'd like me to, I'll stand guard outside your room to protect you from ghosts.'

She looked at me and blinked and I got this feeling that the whole thing was happening in slow motion, the air became more airy, the silence more silent, I felt I was walking through water and that everything changed as I got closer to her bed which was lit up by this light streaming down from nowhere.

'Hang on a minute, Egghead: I'm going to be guarding Peggy!'

Popcorn was standing in the doorway, or rather he was filling the whole doorway. I started shaking. If he was mounting the guard it was bound to be effective, no ghosts would be able to get past that.

Popcorn winked at Peggy.

'Hey, Peggy? We're friends, you and me, aren't we?'

Peggy looked at the ceiling. Popcorn took this as

confirmation and dragged me outside.

'If you want a girl, you can have Sandrine. Peggy's spoken for.'

'How come?'

'Because I was here before you. If you don't like it we can fight.'

'No, actually, I'm really happy.'

I was a bit tired and I went and sat in the games room. And there, in fact, was Sandrine. Sandrine's got leukaemia, like me, except that her treatment seems to be working. We call her Cleopatra because she's got a black wig, it's really shiny, dead straight hair with a fringe and it makes her look like Cleopatra. She looks at me and bursts her bubble of chewing gum.

'You can kiss me if you like.'

'Why, isn't the chewing gum enough?'

'You wouldn't even know how, loser. I bet you've never done it.'

'Oh, that's a good one. I can tell you, at fifteen, I've already done it plenty of times.'

'Are you fifteen?' she asks, surprised.

I check my watch.

'Yes. And the rest.'

'I've always dreamed of being kissed by a big boy of fifteen.'

'It's pretty tempting, you're right,' I tell her.

Then she makes this incredible face with her lips all pushed forward like one of those little suction pads squished onto a window, and I realise she's waiting to be kissed.

I turn round and see all my friends are watching me. There's no way I can back down. I've got to be a man. The time has come.

I go up to her and kiss her. She hangs onto me with her arms, I can't break free now, it's all wet and then suddenly, without any warning, she passes me her chewing gum. I was so surprised I swallowed it whole. I was furious.

That was when someone patted me on the back. Bad luck always comes in threes: my parents. It was Sunday and I'd forgotten!

'Are you going to introduce us to your girlfriend, Oscar?'

'She's not my girlfriend.'

'Will you introduce us, anyway?'

'Sandrine. My parents. Sandrine.'

'Delighted to meet you,' Cleopatra said in a sugary little voice.

I could have strangled her.

'Would you like Sandrine to come to your room with us?'

'No. Sandrine's staying here.'

When I got back to my bed I realised I was tired and I slept for a bit. I didn't want to talk to them, anyway.

When I woke up, obviously they'd brought me some presents. Since I've been in hospital full-time, my parents have had problems with conversation, so they bring me presents and we spend rubbish afternoons reading instructions and rules for games. My father's absolutely fearless with leaflets: even when they're in Turkish or Japanese he doesn't give up, he latches onto the diagram. He's the world champion of the ruined Sunday afternoon.

Today he brought me a CD player. Now there I couldn't criticise him even if I'd wanted to.

'Didn't you come yesterday?'

'Yesterday? Why would we? We can only come on Sundays. What makes you say that?'

'Someone saw your car in the car park.'

'There's more than one red Jeep in the world. Cars are interchangeable you know.'

'Yup. Not like parents. Pity.'

With that I really froze them to the spot. Then I picked up the CD player and listened to *The Nutcracker* twice, without stopping, in front of them. Two hours in which they couldn't say a thing. Well done them.

'Do you like it?'

'Yup. I'm tired.'

They realised they should leave. They felt terrible. They couldn't make up their minds. I could tell they wanted to say something to me but they couldn't manage it. It was good seeing them suffering, them too.

Then my mother rushed over to me and hugged me really hard, too hard, and she said in a shaky voice:

'I love you, my little Oscar, I love you so much.'

I felt like resisting her but at the last minute I let her do it. It reminded me of before, of when big hugs were so straightforward, when she didn't sound heartbroken when she told me she loved me.

After that I must have slept for a bit.

Granny Rose is the champion of waking up time. She always gets to the start line just as I open my eyes. And she always smiles that exact minute.

'So, how were your parents?'

'Rubbish as usual. Well, they gave me *The Nutcracker*.'

'Nutcracker? That's odd. I used to have a friend called that. A hell of a champion. She used to break her opponents' necks between her thighs. What about Peggy Blue, did you go and see her?'

'Don't want to talk about it. She's engaged to Popcorn.'

'Did she tell you that?'

'No, he did.'

'He's just bluffing!'

'I don't think so. I'm sure she likes him more than me. He's bigger, more reassuring.'

'It's all bluff, I tell you! I looked like a little mouse in the ring, but I beat wrestlers who looked like whales and hippopotamuses. Look, there was Plum Pudding, the Irish girl, 150kg on an empty stomach and in her knickers before having her Guinness, forearms the size of my thighs, biceps like prize hams, legs I couldn't get my arms round. No waist, nothing to get hold of. Unbeatable!'

'How did you do it?'

'When you can't get a hold, that means they're all round and they roll. I made her run about, to tire her out, then I rolled her over, rolled the Plum Pudding. They had to use a winch to get her back up. Now, it's true, Oscar, you've got a small frame and you're not exactly a beefcake, but seduction isn't just to do with meat and bones, it's also to do with what's in your heart. And that's one of your strong points, what's in your heart.'

'Me?'

'Go and see Peggy Blue and tell her what you're feeling.'

'I'm a bit tired.'

'Tired? How old are you at the moment? Eighteen? People aren't tired at eighteen.'

Granny Rose's got a way of talking which gives you energy.

It was dark outside, noises seemed to echo more loudly in the half light, the moon was reflected in the lino along the corridor.

I went into Peggy's room and handed her my CD player.

'Here. Listen to the "Waltz of the Snowflakes". It's so pretty it made me think of you.'

Peggy listened to the 'Waltz of the Snowflakes'. She smiled as if that waltz had been an old friend whispering funny stories in her ear.

She handed the machine back to me and said:

'It's beautiful.'

It was the first thing she'd said. That's a pretty good first thing to say, don't you think?

'Peggy Blue, I wanted to tell you: I don't want you to have your operation. You're beautiful just the way you are. You're beautiful in blue.'

And I could tell she really liked that. That's not why I said it, but it was obvious she liked it.

'I'd like you to be the one who protects me from the ghosts, Oscar.'

'You can count on me, Peggy.'

I was really proud. At last, I was the one who'd won!

'Kiss me.'

That's really a girl thing, kissing, they seem to need it. But Peggy's not like Cleopatra, she's not nasty, she just tilted her cheek towards me and it's true, it did make me feel all warm too, when I kissed her.

'Goodnight, Peggy.'

'Goodnight, Oscar.'

So there you are, God, that was my day. I can see why people say the teenage years are so difficult. They're tough. But it actually all sorts itself out when you hit twenty. Now I'd like to tell you my daily request: I'd like Peggy and me to get married. I'm not sure if marriage is a mind thing, if it's in your department. Do you do that sort of wish, marriage bureau wishes? If you haven't got that in stock, let me know quickly so that I can find someone who does. I don't want to rush you but I should point out that I haven't got much time. So: Oscar and Peggy Blue getting married. Yes or no. See if it's something you do – it would be a big help for me.

Till tomorrow, love
Oscar

PS By the way, what is your address actually?

Dear God

It's happened, I'm married. It's the 21st of December, I'm heading for thirty and I've got married. Peggy Blue and I decided we'd see about children later. Actually, I don't think she's ready.

It happened last night.

At about one o'clock in the morning I heard Peggy Blue cry out. I sat bolt upright in bed. The ghosts! Peggy Blue was being tortured by ghosts and I'd promised to stand guard over her. She was going to realise I was a loser, she would never speak to me again, and she'd be right.

I got up and walked towards the screaming. When I got to Peggy's room I saw her sitting on her bed watching me coming towards her with this surprised look on her face. I must have looked pretty amazed too because I suddenly had Peggy Blue in front of me, staring at me with her mouth closed, but I could still hear the screams.

So I carried on to the next door and I realised it was Bacon squirming in his bed because of the burns. It made me feel guilty for a moment, I thought of the day I set fire to the house, the cat, the dog and I even fried the goldfish – well, I think they must have boiled, actually. I thought about what they must have been through and I told myself that, in the end, it was just as well they stayed there and died rather than going on living with the memories and the burns, like Bacon, in spite of his skin grafts and his creams.

Bacon curled up into a ball and stopped groaning. I went back to Peggy Blue.

'So it wasn't you, Peggy? I always thought it was you who cried out in the night.'

'And I always thought it was you.'

We couldn't get over what had happened and what we'd told each other: in fact, we'd both been thinking about each other for a long time.

Peggy Blue went even bluer, and that means she's really embarrassed.

'What are you doing, now, Oscar?'

'What about you, Peggy?'

It's incredible how much we've got in common, the same thoughts, the same questions.

'Do you want to sleep with me?'

Girls, they really are incredible. If I'd tried to say something like that, it would have taken me hours, weeks, months of chewing it over in my head before I could get it out. And there she was saying it so naturally, so simply.

'OK.'

So I got into her bed. It was a bit of a squeeze but we had a wonderful night. Peggy Blue smells of hazelnuts and her skin's as soft as mine is on the inside of my arms, but with her it's all over. We slept a lot, dreamed a lot, we held each other close, we told each other everything about ourselves.

Mind you, when Mrs Gommette, the charge nurse, found us together in the morning, there was a terrible scene. She started shouting, the night nurse started shouting, they shouted at each other, then at Peggy, then at me, doors were slammed, they called the others as witnesses, they called us 'poor little things' when we didn't feel sorry for ourselves at all, and it took Granny Rose to put an end to the whole performance.

'Can't you bloody well leave these children in peace? What's more important, the patients or the regulations? I don't give a stuff about your regulations, you know where you can put them. Now, let's have some silence. You can tear each other's hair out somewhere else. This isn't the place, please!'

You couldn't argue with that, just like everything Granny Rose said. She took me back to my room and I slept for a bit.

When I woke up we had a chat.

'So, is this serious then, Oscar, with Peggy?'

'Mega serious, Granny Rose. I'm just so happy. We got married last night.'

'Married?'

'Yes. We did everything men and women do when they're married.'

'Really?'

'Who do you think I am? I'm – what's the time? – I'm over twenty, I can do what I like, can't I?'

'Of course.'

'And, anyway, all the stuff that I used to find disgusting before, when I was young, the kissing and cuddling, well I liked it in the end. It's funny how you change isn't it?'

'I'm so happy for you, Oscar. You're really growing up.'

'There's only one thing we didn't do and that's kissing with tongues. Peggy Blue was worried she'd have babies. What do you think?'

'I think she's right.'

'Really? Can you have babies if you kiss on the mouth? Because, if you can, I'm going to have some with Cleopatra.'

'Calm down, Oscar, it's actually quite unlikely. Very unlikely.'

She seemed to be pretty sure of what she was saying, and that calmed me down a bit because I can tell you, God, but only you, that with Peggy Blue we did once, maybe twice, maybe more, we did do the tongues.

I slept for a bit then Granny Rose and I had lunch together and I started to feel better.

'I can't believe how tired I was this morning.'

'It's pretty normal. When people are in their early twenties they go out at night, they party, they have a hectic lifestyle and they don't look after themselves enough. You have to pay for it. How about going to see God?'

'Ah, at last, have you got his address?'

'I think he's in the chapel.'

Granny Rose dressed me up as if we were setting off for the North Pole, she took me in her arms and took me to the chapel which is at the far end of the hospital grounds, beyond the frozen lawns, well, I won't bother telling you where it is, seeing as it's where you live.

It gave me quite a shock when I saw the statue of you, I mean when I saw the state you were in, practically naked and really skinny on your cross, with wounds all over the place, your head bleeding from the thorns and lolling because your neck couldn't even hold it up any more. It reminded me of me. It made me feel angry. If I was God, like you, I wouldn't have let them do it.

'Come on, Granny Rose: you were a wrestler, you were a great champion, surely you're not going to put your trust in that!'

'Why not, Oscar? Would you put more faith in God if he looked like a body-builder with plenty of meat on his bones, bulging muscles, oiled skin, a short hair-cut and skimpy flattering pants?'

'Well ...'

'Think about it, Oscar. Who do you feel closer to? A God who doesn't feel anything or a God who suffers?'

'A God who suffers, obviously. But if I was him, if I was God, if, like him, I could change things, I would have avoided the suffering.'

'No one can avoid suffering. Not God, not you. Not your parents and not me.'

'Right, OK. But why does there have to be any suffering?'

'That's just it. There's suffering and suffering. Look at his face more closely. Think about it. Does he look as if he's suffering?'

'No. It's strange. He doesn't look as if it hurts.'

'There then. You've got to distinguish between two different kinds of pain, Oscar, my little man, physical suffering and moral suffering. With physical suffering, we just have to take it, but we choose moral suffering.'

'I don't understand.'

'If someone drives nails through your wrists or your feet, you can't help feeling pain. You take it. On the other hand, the idea of dying doesn't have to hurt you. You don't know what it's like. So it's up to you.'

'Do you actually know anyone who's happy at the thought of dying?'

'Yes, I do. My mother was like that. She smiled in anticipation on her death bed, as if it was a treat, she was impatient, she couldn't wait to see what would happen.'

I couldn't argue with her now. I wanted to hear the rest so I waited for a while, thinking about what she'd said.

'But most people don't have any curiosity. They cling on to what they've got, like a flea in a bald man's ear. Take Plum Pudding, for example, my Irish rival, 150kg on an empty stomach and in her knickers before having her Guinness. She always used to say: 'I'm sorry but I'm not going to die, I don't go along with that, I didn't sign up for it.' She was wrong. No one told her life was meant to go on for ever, no one did! She went on stubbornly believing it, she rebelled, refused to contemplate passing, she went crazy over it, got depressed, lost weight, had to stop the work, she was down to just 35kg, she looked like a little fish bone and she just fell apart. You see, she died anyway, like everyone else, but the thought of dying ruined her life.'

'She was thick, that Plum Pudding, Granny Rose.'

'Thick as two short planks. But there's an awful lot of them about, short planks, I mean. A hell of a lot.'

And I nodded my head then too, because I pretty much agreed with her.

'People are frightened of dying because they're afraid of the unknown. But that's just it, what is the unknown? I don't think you should be frightened, Oscar, you should have faith in it. Look at God's face on the cross: he's suffering the physical pain, but he's not feeling any moral pain because he has faith. And, as a result, the nails actually hurt less. He keeps thinking: it hurts but it isn't evil. There! That's the advantage of faith. I wanted to show you that.'

'OK, Granny Rose, when I'm scared, I'll make myself have faith.'

She kissed me. Actually, it was nice being in that deserted church with you, God, looking so peaceful.

When we got back I slept for a long time. I get more and more tired. It's like I can't get enough sleep. When I woke up I told Granny Rose:

'I'm not really afraid of the unknown. It's just I don't want to lose the things I do know.'

'I'm like you, Oscar. How about asking Peggy Blue to come and have tea with us?'

Peggy Blue had tea with us, she got on very well with Granny Rose, and we had a good laugh when Granny Rose told us about her fight with the Slammer Sisters, they were triplets who passed themselves off as one person. After each round, the Slammer who'd exhausted her opponent by running around all over the place would hop out of the ring saying she needed to do a wee. She would rush to the Ladies' and one of her sisters would come out fresh and ready for the next round. And so on. Everyone thought there was only one Slammer, that she was just tireless. Granny Rose found out about their little trick, locked the two stand-ins in the Ladies' and threw the key out of the window, then she got the better of the one left in the ring. It's clever stuff, wrestling.

Then Granny Rose left. The nurses kept an eye on Peggy Blue and me as if we were a couple of bombs about to go off. I mean, shit, I am thirty! Peggy Blue promised me that tonight she would come to my room as soon as she could, so I promised in return that I wouldn't do the tongue thing this time.

It's true, having children isn't everything. Apart from anything else, you've got to have the time to bring them up.

So, there you are, God. I don't know what to ask you for this evening because it's been a good day. Oh yes I do. Could you arrange for Peggy Blue's operation to go well tomorrow. Not like mine, if you see what I mean.

Till tomorrow, love
Oscar

PS Operations aren't mind things, it may not be one of your lines. So could you make it so that, whatever happens in the operation, Peggy Blue takes it well. I'm counting on you.

Dear God

Peggy Blue had her operation today. I've had a terrible ten years. The thirties are a tough time, it's all worry and responsibility.

In the end, Peggy couldn't come and join me in the night because Mrs Ducru, the night nurse, stayed in Peggy's room to get her ready for the anaesthetic. They wheeled her away at about eight o'clock. It made my heart feel all tight seeing Peggy go past on that rolling bed, you could hardly see her under the green sheets because she's so small and thin.

Granny Rose held my hand so that I didn't get too upset.

'Granny Rose, why does your God let this sort of thing happen, people like Peggy and me?'

'It's a good thing he does make you, little man, because life wouldn't be anything like so good without you.'

'No. You don't understand. Why does God let us be ill? Either he's nasty, or he's not brilliant at what he does.'

'Oscar, illness is like death. It's a fact. It's not a punishment.'

'It shows that you're not ill!'

'What would you know about that, Oscar?'

Well, that brought me up short. I'd never thought that Granny Rose – who's always so available and always so attentive – could have problems of her own.

'You mustn't hide things from me, Granny Rose, you can tell me everything. I'm at least thirty two, I've got cancer and a wife in the operating theatre, so I know quite a lot about life.'

'I love you, Oscar.'

'Me too. How can I help you if you've got problems? Would you like me to adopt you?'

'Adopt me?'

'Yes, I've already adopted Bernard, when I saw how sad he was.'

'Who's Bernard?'

'My teddy. There. In the wardrobe. On the shelf. He's my old teddy, he hasn't got his eyes any more, or a mouth, or a nose, he's lost half his stuffing and he's got scars all over the place. He's a bit like you. I adopted him the evening my stupid parents brought me a new teddy. As if I would agree to have a new teddy! They might as well replace me with a new brother while they're at it! Since then, I've adopted him. I'll leave him everything I've got, I'll leave it to Bernard. I'd like to adopt you too, if it would make you feel better.'

'Yes. I'd really like that. I think that would make me feel much better, Oscar.'

'Well then, let's shake on it, Granny Rose.'

Then we went and got Peggy's room ready, we brought

chocolates and put flowers in there for when she came back.

After that I slept. It's incredible how much I sleep at the moment.

Towards the end of the afternoon, Granny Rose woke me to say that Peggy Blue had come back and that the operation had been a success.

We went to see her together. Her parents were by her bedside. I don't know who'd told them, Peggy or Granny Rose, but they seemed to know who I was, they treated me with great respect and put a chair between them so that I could watch my wife with my parents-in-law.

I was happy because Peggy was still bluish. Dr Düsseldorf came by, rubbed his eyebrows and said it would change in the next few hours. I looked at Peggy's mother who isn't blue but is still very pretty and I thought that Peggy, my wife, could actually be whatever colour she liked, I'd still love her just as much.

Peggy opened her eyes, smiled at us, I mean at me and at her parents, then went back to sleep.

That reassured her parents but they had to go.

'We'll entrust our daughter to you,' they told me. 'We know we can count on you.'

With Granny Rose there, I hung on until Peggy opened her eyes again, then I went and had a rest in my room.

Now that I'm coming to the end of this letter, I can see that it's been a good day today, in the end. A family day. I've adopted Granny Rose, I've got on really well with my in-laws and I've got my wife back in good health even if, towards eleven o'clock, she did start to go pink.

Till tomorrow, love
Oscar

PS No wish today. That'll give you a rest.

Dear God

Today I've gone from forty to fifty and I've done nothing but make stupid mistakes.

I'll go over it quickly because it's not worth spending time on it. Peggy Blue's fine but Cleopatra – sent by Popcorn who can't bloody stand me any more – came and sneaked to her that I'd kissed her on the mouth.

Because of that, Peggy told me that it was over between us. I argued and said that, with Cleopatra, it had been a mistake when I was very young, way before her time, and she couldn't make me pay for my past all my life.

But she stood her ground. She even made friends with Cleopatra to annoy me, and I heard them giggling together.

So when Brigitte came along – she's the Down's Syndrome girl who clings to everyone because that's what Down's people do, they're affectionate – when she came to say hello to me in my room, I let her kiss me all over. She was so happy I let her, she was like a dog greeting its master. The problem was Einstein was in the corridor. He may have water on his brain but there's nothing wrong with his eyesight. He saw everything, and went and told Peggy and Cleopatra. Now the whole floor's calling me a womaniser, and I haven't even left my room.

'I don't know what came over me, Granny Rose, with Brigitte ...'

'It's a mid-life crisis, Oscar. Men are like that between forty-five and fifty, they want reassurance, they want to check they still appeal to other women, not just the one they love.'

'Right, OK, so I'm normal but I'm also pretty stupid, aren't I?'

'Yes. You're completely normal.'

'What should I do?'

'Who do you love?'

'Peggy. Just Peggy.'

'Well, tell her that. A first relationship can be fragile, always under threat, but you have to fight to keep it going if it's the right one.'

Tomorrow is Christmas, God. I'd never realised before that it's your birthday. Can you make it so that I get back together with Peggy because, I don't know if it's because of that, but I'm feeling very sad this evening and I haven't got the heart to do anything any more.

Till tomorrow, love
Oscar

PS Now that we're friends, what would you like me to give you for your birthday?

Dear God

At eight o'clock this morning I told Peggy Blue that I loved her, I loved only her and I couldn't imagine my life without her. She started to cry and she admitted that I'd taken a terrible weight off her shoulders because she only loved me, too, and that she would never find anyone else, especially now she was pink.

Then, it was odd, we ended up both crying but it was very nice. It's great, being in a relationship. Specially in your fifties when you've been through quite a lot.

As it struck ten o'clock, I properly realised that it was

Christmas, that I couldn't stay with Peggy because her family – brothers, uncles, nephews and cousins – were going to pitch up in her room, and that I was going to have to put up with my parents. What were they going to give me now? Books in Kurdish? A box of instruction leaflets? A picture of me from when I was well? With a couple of idiots like them – who've got the IQ of a pair of bin-bags – there were all sorts of threats looming on the horizon, I had everything to fear and I could be sure of only one thing: I was going to have a rubbish day.

I made my mind up very quickly and planned my escape. A bit of bartering: my toys to Einstein, my duvet to Bacon and my sweets to Popcorn. A bit of observation: Granny Rose always went to the cloakroom before leaving. A bit of estimation: my parents would never get here before twelve. Everything went well: at half past eleven, Granny Rose kissed me and said she hoped I had a nice Christmas with my parents, then she disappeared down to the cloakroom. I whistled. Popcorn, Einstein and Bacon quickly got me dressed, helped me downstairs and carried me to Granny Rose's old banger – which must have been made before cars were even invented. Popcorn (who's very good at opening cars because he was lucky enough to be brought up on a really rough estate) picked the lock on one of the back doors, and they threw me onto the floor between the front and rear seats. Then they went back into the building and no one even knew they'd been gone.

After a little while Granny Rose got into her car, made it splutter ten or fifteen times before it started, then set off at break-neck speed. Ancient old bangers like that are great, they make such a racket you feel you're going really quickly and they throw you around like a fun-fair ride.

The problem was Granny Rose must have learned to drive from a stunt man: she didn't pay any attention to red lights, pavements or roundabouts so, from time to time, the car actually took off. It was a pretty rough ride in the cabin, she did a lot of beeping and, from the point of view of vocabulary, it was an enriching experience: she hurled all sorts of terrible insults at the enemies who got in her way and, once again, I thought how wrestling was a good preparation for life.

I'd been planning to pop up and say 'Hello, Granny Rose' when we arrived, but it went on so long – the obstacle course to get to her house – that I must have gone to sleep.

Anyway, when I woke up it was dark, it was cold and very quiet, and there I was all alone, lying on the damp carpeting. That was when I first realised I might have made a mistake.

I got out of the car and it started to snow. But it was nothing like as nice as the 'Waltz of the Snowflakes' from *The Nutcracker*. My teeth were leaping about all on their own.

I saw a big house with the lights on, and started walking towards it, but it was hard work. I had to jump so high to reach the doorbell that I collapsed on the doormat.

That's where Granny Rose found me.

'But ... but ...,' she started to say.

Then she leaned over me and whispered:

'My darling.'

So I thought maybe I hadn't made a mistake.

She carried me into her sitting-room where she'd got a big Christmas tree all winking with lights. I couldn't believe how lovely it was in Granny Rose's house. She warmed me up by the fire and we had a big mug of hot chocolate. I guessed she wanted to check I was all right first before telling me off. So, you see, I made sure I took my time recovering, and it wasn't difficult, actually, because I'm so tired at the moment.

'Everyone's looking for you at the hospital, Oscar. It's pandemonium. Your parents are frantic. They've contacted the police.'

'That doesn't surprise me, knowing them. Are they really so stupid they think I'll love them once I've got handcuffs on ...'

'Why do you resent them so much?'

'They're frightened of me. They can't bring themselves to speak to me. And the less they speak to me, the more like a monster they make me feel. Why are they so scared of me? Am I really that ugly? Do I smell? Have I gone mad without realising it?'

'They're not frightened of you, Oscar. They're frightened of the illness.'

'My illness is part of me. They shouldn't behave differently because I'm ill. Or can they only love me when I'm well?'

'They love you, Oscar. They told me so.'

'Do you speak to them?'

'Yes. They're very jealous that we get on so well. No, not jealous, sad. Sad they can't manage it too.'

I shrugged my shoulders but I was already not feeling so angry. Granny Rose made me another mug of chocolate.

'You know, Oscar, you're going to die one day... but your parents are going to die too.'

I was amazed by what she'd just said. I'd never thought of it.

'Yes. They're going to die too. All on their own. And full of terrible remorse because they couldn't make up with their only child, their Oscar who they adored.'

'Don't say things like that, Granny Rose, it's bloody depressing.'

'Think about them, Oscar. You understand that you're going to die because you're a very intelligent boy. But you don't understand that you're not the only one who's going to die. Everyone dies. Your parents will one day. I will one day.'

'Yes. But still, I am going first.'

'That's true. You're going first. But then, just because you're going first, does that give you every right? Including the right to forget about everyone else?'

'I understand, Granny Rose, call them.'

So, there you are, God, I'll go over what happened next quickly because my wrist is getting tired. Granny Rose got in touch with the hospital and they got in touch with my parents, and they came over to Granny Rose's house and we had Christmas together.

When my parents arrived I said:

'I'm sorry. I'd forgotten that you were going to die one day too.'

I don't know what it unlocked inside them, that sentence, but after that they were just like before and we had a brilliant Christmas.

When we were having pudding Granny Rose wanted to put the television on to watch midnight mass and a wrestling match she'd recorded. She said she's been doing it for years, saving a wrestling match to watch before midnight mass to limber her up, it had become a habit and it would make her happy. So we all watched a fight that she'd been saving. It was fantastic: Mephista against Joan of Arc! Swimming costumes and thigh boots! Great strapping women! Dad kept saying, all red in the face and seeming to enjoy it, the wrestling, I mean. You can't imagine how many times they smacked each other in the face. I would have died a hundred times in a fight like that. It's all down to training, Granny Rose told me, with punches in the face – the more you take, the more you can take. You always have to hope. In the end it was Joan of Arc who won when actually, at the beginning, you wouldn't have thought she could: you must have liked that.

By the way, happy birthday, God. Granny Rose (who's just tucked me up in her eldest son's bed – he's a vet in the Congo with the elephants) said that me making up with my parents was a great birthday present for you. But, to be honest, I think it's a bit borderline as a present. Still if Granny Rose says so, and her being an old friend of yours ...

Till tomorrow, love
Oscar

PS I forgot my wish: for my parents always to be like this evening. And me too. It was a brilliant Christmas, specially Mephista against Joan of Arc. Sorry about midnight mass, I gave up before then.

Dear God

I'm over sixty and I'm paying the price for everything I did yesterday evening. I haven't been feeling that great today.

It was nice coming back home, to the hospital. You get like that when you're old, you don't like travelling any more. I definitely don't want to go away again.

What I didn't tell you in my letter yesterday was that in Granny Rose's house there was a statue of Peggy Blue on some shelves by the stairs. I swear it. Exactly like her, in plaster, with the same sweet face and the same blue colour for the clothes and skin. Granny Rose says it's the Virgin Mary (your mother, if I've got things straight), a Madonna which has been in her family several generations. She agreed to give it to me. I've put it on my bedside table. It'll end up back in Granny Rose's family, anyway, because I've adopted her.

Peggy Blue's much better. She came to see me in a wheelchair. She couldn't see the likeness with the statue but we had a lovely time together. We held hands and listened to *The Nutcracker*, and it reminded us of the good times.

I won't say any more now because I'm finding the pen quite heavy. Everyone here is ill, even Dr Düsseldorf because of all the chocolates, foie gras, marrons glacés and champagne all the parents give to the nursing staff. I'd really like it if you came to see me.

Till tomorrow, love
Oscar

Dear God

Today I went from seventy to eighty years old, and I've done a lot of thinking.

First, I used Granny Rose's Christmas present. I don't know if I told you about it? It's a plant from the Sahara which lives its whole life in just one day. As soon as the seed gets some water it germinates, it gets a stalk, grows leaves, produces a flower, makes seeds, wilts and shrivels back up and – ta-da! – it's all over by the evening. It's a cool present, thank you for inventing it. We watered it at seven o'clock this morning, Granny Rose, my parents and me – by the way, I don't know if I told you this, they're living with Granny Rose at the moment because it's not so far – and I watched its whole life. I found it moving. I know it's a pretty sickly, stingy sort of flower (it's not a patch on a baobab!) but it got on with its job being a plant, bravely like a grown-up, and it did it in front of us all day, without stopping.

With Peggy Blue I read a lot of the Medical Dictionary. It's her favourite book. She's fascinated by illnesses and she likes working out which ones she could have later. I looked for the words that mattered to me: 'Life', 'Death', 'Faith' and 'God'. You're not going to believe this but they weren't in it! Mind you, at least that proves they're not illnesses – life, death, faith and you. Which is good news, really. Still, in a serious book like that there should be answers to the most serious questions of all, shouldn't there?

'Granny Rose, I get the feeling that the Medical Dictionary only has specific things, problems that could happen to one person or another. But there aren't the things that affect us all: Life, Death, Faith and God.'

'Maybe you should look at a Dictionary of Philosophy, Oscar. Mind you, even if you do find the ideas you're looking for, you're likely to be disappointed. It would give you several very different answers for each concept.'

'How come?'

'The most interesting questions will always be questions. They contain mysteries. For every reply there has to be a "maybe". Only boring questions have definitive answers.'

'You mean that there isn't a solution to "Life"?'

'I mean there are several solutions to "Life", and therefore no solution.'

'Well, this is what I think, Granny Rose, there's no solution to life except to live it.'

Dr Düsseldorf came by to see us. He traipsed in with his hangdog expression which is even more exaggerated with those great black eyebrows.

'Do you comb your eyebrows, Dr Düsseldorf?' I asked him.

He looked all round, really surprised, and I think he was checking with Granny Rose and my parents to see if he'd heard me right. Eventually, he said yes in a choked voice.

'Don't make that face, Dr Düsseldorf. Listen, I'm going to be absolutely frank because I've always done everything I should on the medicine side of things and you've been straight down the line on the illness side. Stop looking so guilty. It's not your fault if you have to give people bad news, tell them illnesses with Latin names and impossible cures. You need to relax. Let yourself go a bit. You're not God the Father. You don't give orders to nature. You're just the repairman. You need to slow down, Dr Düsseldorf, ease off the pressure and not take so much responsibility yourself, or you won't be able to keep this job up for long. I mean, look at your face already.'

As he listened, Dr Düsseldorf looked like he was swallowing an egg whole. Then he smiled, a real smile, and he hugged me.

'You're right, Oscar. Thank you for telling me that.'

'It's a pleasure, Doctor. At your service. Call again whenever you like!'

So, there you are, God. Mind you, I'm still waiting for you to visit. Come on. Don't be shy. Please come, even if there are quite a few people with me at the moment. It would really make me happy.

Till tomorrow, love
Oscar

Dear God

Peggy Blue has left. She's gone home to her parents. I'm not stupid, I know I'll never see her again.

I'm not going to write to you because I'm too sad. We spent our lives together, Peggy and I, and now I'm all on my own, bald, weak and tired, lying in my bed. It's horrible growing old.

I don't like you any more today.

Oscar

Dear God

Thanks for coming.

You chose just the right moment because I wasn't feeling at all good. Maybe you were also a bit upset because of my letter yesterday ...

When I woke up I thought about being ninety years old, and I turned to look at the window to watch the snow.

And right then I could tell you were coming. It was morning and I was all alone on the Earth. It was so early that the birds were still asleep, Mrs Ducru (the night nurse) must have been having a snooze and you were trying to get the dawn together. You were having a bit of trouble but you kept at it. The sky was getting lighter. You were blowing up the air with whites, greys and blues, pushing back the darkness and bringing the world back to life. You didn't give up. That's when I understood the difference between you and us: you're Mr Indefatigable! The one who never gets tired, always at his work. And here's day! And here's night! And here's spring! And here's winter! And here's Peggy Blue! And here's Oscar! And here's Granny Rose! So much energy!

I knew you were there. That you were telling me your secret: look at the world every day as if it were the first time.

So I took your advice and I tried to do it. The first time. I looked at the light, the colours, the trees, the birds and the animals. I felt the air going through my nostrils and making me breathe. I heard voices floating up in the corridor as if they were under the vaulted roof of a cathedral. I felt alive. I shuddered with sheer joy. The happiness of existing. I was dazzled.

Thank you, God, for doing that for me. I felt as if you were taking me by the hand and taking me into the heart of the mystery to look at the mystery. Thank you.

Till tomorrow, love
Oscar

PS My wish: could you do the first-time thing for my parents? I think Granny Rose already knows it. And Peggy, too, if you have time ...

Dear God

I'm a hundred years old today. Like Granny Rose. I sleep a lot but I feel good.

I tried to explain to my parents that life was a strange present. At first we overestimate it, this present: we think we've been given eternal life. Afterwards we under-estimate it, we think it's rubbish, too short, we're almost prepared to chuck it away. In the end we realise it wasn't a present, just a loan. So then we try to deserve it. And I'm a hundred so I know what I'm talking about. The older we get the more likely we are to appreciate life. We have to refine our tastes, become artists. Any old fool can enjoy life at ten or twenty, but when you get to a hundred, when you can no longer move, you have to put your brains to work.

I don't know if I really convinced them.

Go and see them. Finish the job. I'm getting a bit tired.

Till tomorrow, love
Oscar

Dear God

A hundred and ten. That's old. I think I'm starting to die.

Oscar

Dear God

The little boy has died.

I will always be a lady in pink but I won't be Granny Rose any more. I was only that to him.

He passed away this morning, in the half hour when his parents and I went to have a cup of coffee. He did it without us. I think he waited till then to spare us. As if he wanted to save us from the violence of seeing him go. In fact he was the one who was watching over us.

My heart's aching, it's heavy, Oscar is in my heart and I can't get him out. I must keep my tears to myself for now, until this evening, because I don't want to compare my pain to the insurmountable agony of his parents.

Thank you for introducing me to Oscar. Thanks to him I was amusing, I invented myths and I even knew a thing or two about wrestling. Thanks to him I laughed and I knew happiness. He helped me believe in you. I am so full of love it's burning, he gave me so much that I've got enough for all the years to come.

Speak to you soon,
Granny Rose

PS For the last three days Oscar had a little sign on his bedside table. I think you should know. It said: 'Only God is allowed to wake me.'